T. RUNT!

A
Silverline™
B O O K S
PRODUCTION
A DIVISION OF
Shadowline™ / image®

T. RUNT!
ISBN: 978-1-60706-074-1
First Printing, June, 2009
Ages 4-8

Written by Derek McCulloch
Illustrated by Jimmie Robinson

Edited by Kristen Simon
Published by Jim Valentino

For Pearl and Zohn.

One quiet Thursday in the late Cretaceous Period, some
shells cracked open and three baby dinosaurs were born.

These weren't just any dinosaurs.

They were tyrannosaurus rex, the terror of all the other dinosaurs.

The first baby tyrannosaur was named Magnus. He had big powerful jaws and great sharp teeth.

The second baby tyrannosaur was named Maxima. She had big hind feet that made smaller animals run whenever she stomped by.

The last baby tyrannosaur
was named Vegrandis.

He was smaller than Magnus.
He was smaller than Maxima.

And he was always last in line when
their mother brought home dinner.

When Maxima sat down under her favorite leafy tree, she didn't look to see if anyone was already there.

HEY!

Vegrandis asked his mother, *"Why do I have to be the smallest one?"*

His mother patted him on the head and said, *"Don't worry. You'll get bigger."*

Vegrandis asked his father the same thing.

His father said, *"Somebody's got to be smallest. It's the law of the jungle."*

That didn't make Vegrandis feel any better. He decided to go for a walk.

As he was coming over a little hill, Vegrandis heard a noisy commotion. He wondered what it was.

Down by the creek, he saw a group of small, furry mammals. They were crowded around one even smaller furry mammal.

Vegrandis was curious. He was used to being pushed around for being small. He had never seen it happen to somebody else.

Vegrandis knew just how the small furry mammal felt. He remembered times when Magnus and Maxima had taken things away from him. Vegrandis started to get angry...

THEY'RE MINE!!

... and the sight of an angry tyrannosaur – even a little tyrannosaur – was something small furry mammals were quick to notice.

For just one moment, the small furry mammal – whose name was Larry – thought that HE had chased off the bigger furry mammals.

YEAH, THAT'S RIGHT! RUN!

It didn't take long for him to realize his mistake.

Vegrandis remembered what his father said about the law of the jungle – that somebody had to be smallest.

He wondered:
"Are you the smallest creature there is?"

"I found these grub worms all by myself," Larry complained, "and those big guys were trying to take them away!"

"Grub worms go great with berries," said Larry. "They're the best breakfast ever!"

Just then, Larry realized that food might not be the best topic of conversation when speaking with a tyrannosaur.

He offered Vegrandis some of his grub worms and was very relieved when Vegrandis said, *"No thanks, I'm not hungry."*

Vegrandis was too busy thinking to eat. He was thinking about big and small.

He was smaller than his brother and sister, but he was bigger than the small furry mammals. He was much bigger than the grub worms. He wasn't the biggest but he wasn't really the smallest, either. Vegrandis thought that maybe he didn't mind being the size he was.

But as time went on, a
funny thing happened.

Vegrandis got bigger.
Magnus and Maxima got bigger too, of course,
but Vegrandis got a LOT bigger.

Magnus and Maxima asked their father, "Why does Vegrandis get to be the biggest one?"

Their father answered, "Somebody's got to be biggest. It's the law of the jungle."

But Vegrandis knew that there's always someone bigger and there's always someone smaller. And even though he was the bigger one now, he treated Magnus and Maxima very nicely, just the way he'd always wanted them to treat him.

As big as Vegrandis got, Larry stayed just the same.
He was always the smallest one of his friends.
But those bigger furry mammals were a lot nicer to him.

Larry thought it was because he always shared his grub worms. But maybe – *just maybe...*

– it had something to do with his new best friend.

T.RUNT! WORD FIND

Fill in the blanks below, and find the words in the puzzle! (Words in the puzzle can be found horizontally, vertically, diagonally, forwards, and backwards.)

1. T. Runt! is a story about a baby tyrannosaur named _____

2. Who has a brother named _____

3. and a sister named _____

4. Their mother has a recipe book for raw _____

5. The baby dinosaur gets picked on because he is _____

6. and is always last in line for _____

7. He makes friends with a small furry mammal named _____

8. Who likes to eat (2 words) _____

9. They all live in the _____ period.

10. The baby dinosaur's father likes to read the (3 words) _____

L	X	S	U	N	G	A	M	A	U	N	D	T	L	P
G	R	U	B	W	O	R	M	S	A	B	S	L	H	Z
S	R	G	F	T	R	R	Y	E	W	E	A	U	B	C
E	S	X	Q	V	X	F	E	Z	D	M	I	E	C	W
M	L	K	A	Q	E	Q	F	J	S	E	G	G	R	H
I	A	N	Y	K	L	G	A	V	H	O	I	J	E	C
T	R	T	K	B	G	H	R	L	E	V	M	N	T	I
K	R	V	P	U	B	O	P	A	O	Q	M	R	A	S
R	Y	C	T	X	O	U	V	W	N	F	A	I	C	J
O	X	M	T	Y	Z	C	Y	V	N	D	X	A	E	V
Y	A	D	B	Y	E	C	U	D	P	J	I	E	O	F
D	H	A	D	R	O	S	A	U	R	G	M	S	U	H
L	I	J	Y	K	X	L	M	F	M	D	A	N	S	O
O	W	P	Q	L	N	L	R	Z	S	S	L	T	E	K
D	I	N	N	E	R	D	U	V	M	X	A	M	H	T

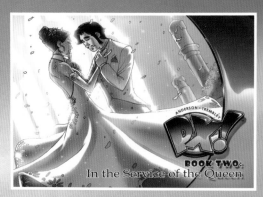

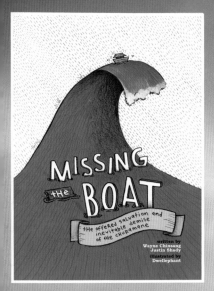

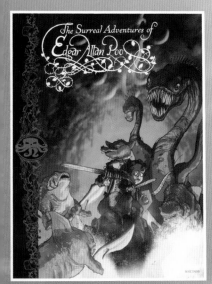

Derek McCulloch is an award-winning writer of graphic novels for grownups. He wanted to make a book that his daughter could read, so he wrote T. Runt! He hopes you like it as much as she did.

Jimmie Robinson is an illustrator of comic books and graphic novels. He is located in California where he tends his cats, feeds birds, and digs in the garden.